Little Patriot Press

Liberty Lee's
Tail of Independence

The unanimouse Declaration of the thirteen united States of America

When in the course of human events it becomes necessary for one people to dissolve the bonds which have connected another, and

By Peter W. Barnes and Cheryl Shaw Barnes

Text copyright © 2012 by Peter W. Barnes
Jacket art and interior illustrations copyright © 2012 by Cheryl Shaw Barnes

Cataloging-in-Publication data on file with the Library of Congress
ISBN 978-1-59698-792-0

Published in the United States by
Regnery Publishing, Inc.
One Massachusetts Avenue, NW
Washington, DC 20001
www.Regnery.com

Manufactured in the United States of America
10 9 8 7 6 5 4 3 2 1

Books are available in quantity for promotional or premium use.
For information on discounts and terms write to Director of Special Sales, Regnery Publishing, Inc.,
One Massachusetts Avenue, NW, Washington, DC, 2001, or call 202-216-0600.

Distributed to the trade by:
Perseus Distribution
387 Park Avenue South
New York, NY 10016

We dedicate this book

to our friend, philanthropist Kenneth E. Behring,
who has in turn dedicated his life to giving mobility and independence
to the physically disabled around the world. Over the past decade
Ken and his Wheelchair Foundation have circled the globe many times over
to deliver more than 850,000 wheelchairs in more than 150 countries.
He has also helped make history come alive for our nation's families
as the major benefactor of the National Museum of American History
at the Smithsonian Institution in Washington, D.C.
We honor Ken as a patriot and a citizen of the world.

—PWB and CSB

★ ★ ★

Find the Eagle hidden in each illustration.

'Twas the Fourth of July and all through the nation,
America celebrated its Declaration
Of its right to be independent and free—
We know the whole tale, my friend Thomas and me!

Over there—Thomas Jefferson, the man on the horse—
Founding Father and our third president, of course.
And I'm right down here with my flag, you can see—
I'm a mouse Yankee Doodle named Liberty Lee!

To begin, let's go back more than 400 years
To meet the first settlers—the first pioneers.
Across the Atlantic from England they came
To seek opportunity, fortune, and fame!

My great-great-great grandfather, Lancaster Lee,
Led many brave mice in a new colony,
In Jamestown, Virginia, as all his friends knew—
Pocahontas and Captain John Smith, to name two!

More and more settlers came, and the colonies grew
To 13—busy places with much work to do.
There were carpenters, shopkeepers, sailors at sea,
And farmers—like my uncle, Hamilton Lee.

At planting tobacco, you'd find no one better—
He worked any farm that would pay him in cheddar!
These were times of great promise—of great hopes and fears—
And for most, these were peaceful and prosperous years.

NEW
HAMPSHIRE

NEW YORK

MASSACHUSETTS

CT.   R.I.

PENNSYLVANIA

NEW
JERSEY

DELAWARE

MARYLAND

VIRGINIA

NORTH
CAROLINA

SOUTH
CAROLINA

GEORGIA

By now, back in England, the King—George the Third—
Watched the colonies prosper and sent them the word:
They should pay more in taxes—send money with speed.
And Parliament, which passed all the laws, fast agreed!

The colonists quickly became very mad!
They yelled the new taxes were unfair—and bad!
The King taxed their sugar, molasses, and teas—
Goodness grief! What was next—macaroni and cheese?!?!?!

We colonists wanted to the send to the King
A message we hoped he would find challenging:
We felt there should never be any taxation
Without, in the government, representation.

When we did not get it, we started to fight!
We dressed up as Indians in Boston one night.
We boarded a ship full of tea in a flash,
Then dumped all the tea in the harbor, ker-splash!

The Continental Congress assembled that fall
In Philadelphia, where we patriots all
Agreed to a list of self-evident facts:
The laws of the King were intolerable acts!

In Lexington and Concord, our soldiers fought back
When the King's Redcoats began to attack!
Our Minutemen forced them to scatter and run—
The American Revolution had begun!

The Continental Congress then met to decide
That our independence could not be denied!
The members appointed young Thomas (and me)
To write a declaration—and make history!

We worked very hard, all day and all night—
We wrote by the fire and by candlelight.
As Franklin and Adams checked in, came and went,
We wrote about "truths" that were self-evident!

After 17 days, amid great expectation,
We gave to the Congress a "draft" declaration.
Then all of the members from each delegation
Checked all the words and—of course—punctuation!

They debated, and then on the 4th of July,
In 1776, they said, "Aye!"—
They voted together, with great dedication,
For liberty, freedom, and starting a nation.

Fifty-six patriots signed right below
The powerful words they decided would show
That these **United States** would forever be
One nation, under God, independent and free!

They pledged all they had to this cause, without fear—
Their lives, sacred honor, and fortunes, so dear.
They declared they would fight and would die for this cause!
Please turn the page now to read the first clause.

There are times, "in the course of human events,"
People want to create their own governments.
That was the purpose of our Declaration,
Which stated the reasons for our separation,

From Britain—our homeland—and a King far away
Who hurt and mistreated us day after day.
"Separate and equal" would be our new station,
To govern ourselves in our very own nation!

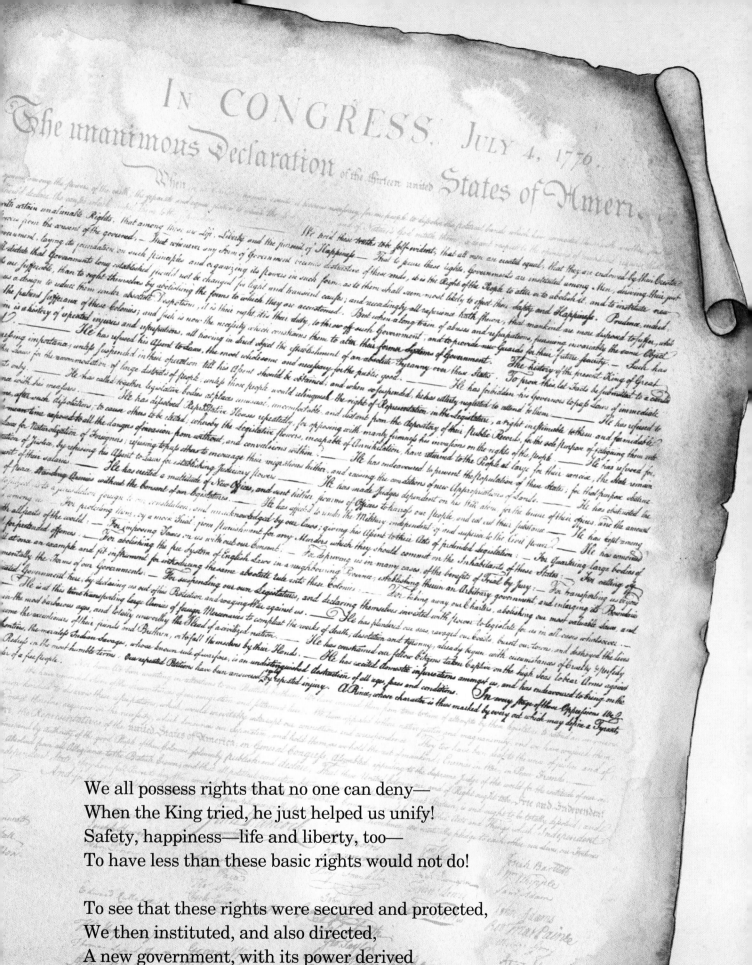

We all possess rights that no one can deny—
When the King tried, he just helped us unify!
Safety, happiness—life and liberty, too—
To have less than these basic rights would not do!

To see that these rights were secured and protected,
We then instituted, and also directed,
A new government, with its power derived
From the people, whose freedoms the King had deprived.

Let a candid world see his offenses revealed!
He decreed honest laws to be stopped or repealed.
His army invaded, waged war, destroyed lives.
He cut off our trade (not much trading survives).

He taxed us unfairly, without our consent;
And trials by jury he sought to prevent.
He ignored our petitions without explanation—
We had to fight back—for our own preservation!

We therefore declare, for the whole world to see,
These colonies are—and of right, ought to be—
With providence, states independent and free,
Their connections to Britain dissolved totally!

Then this Declaration and all that was in it
Was signed by John Hancock—and by Button Gwinnett!
And Benjamin Franklin, John Adams, George Read—
Fifty-one more Founding Fathers agreed!

The new Declaration was read through the land—
The colonists rejoiced, with their freedom at hand!
They shouted the news from every rooftop and steeple—
A government OF, BY, and FOR the people!

It would not be easy. We were now at war.
But it was a dream that was worth fighting for!
It would take faith and courage, and great sacrifice,
From all of our citizens—including us mice!

We fought many battles, north and south, in six years—
A thousand or more—with our blood, sweat, and tears!

10

Saratoga, NY
September 19 and October 7, 1777

The Continental Army won a major victory over the British—a turning point of the war that brought French support for America.

8

Bennington, VT
August 16, 1777

The patriot militia defeated British forces trying to raid the town for supplies.

6

Trenton, NJ
December 26, 1776

General Washington and his troops crossed the Delaware River in a surprise attack on Hessian soldiers fighting for the British.

9

Brandywine, PA
September 11, 1777

Germantown, PA
October 4, 1777

The Continental Army fought to protect Philadelphia from British capture but failed.

7

Princeton, NJ
January 3, 1777

The Continental Army defeated the British garrison. More colonists began to enlist.

12

Monmouth Courthouse, NJ
June 28, 1778

After Valley Forge, a better-trained Continental Army fought the British to a draw. Last major battle of the North.

11

Valley Forge, PA
December 19, 1777–June 19, 1778

General Washington set up winter camp to rest and train his troops.

▼ SOUTHERN BATTLES ▼ 1775–1783

13

Savannah, GA
December 29, 1778

The British began the southern campaign, defeated the patriot militia, and captured the city.

14

Charleston, SC
April 2–May 12, 1780

The British captured this strategic port city after heavy bombardment.

Then our troops, led by General George Washington,
Defeated the British at Yorktown! We won!

2
Fort Ticonderoga, NY
May 10, 1775
Vermont militia captured the British outpost, providing cannons and supplies for the Continental Army.

3
Bunker Hill, MA
June 17, 1775
The colonial militia held off the British near Boston, leading the Americans to create the Continental Army.

1
Lexington and Concord, MA
April 19, 1775
The first shots were fired between British Redcoats and American Minutemen.

5
Long Island, NY
August 27–29, 1776
The first major battle of the war. The British defeated the Continental Army, led by General Washington. The Army retreated to New York.

NORTHERN BATTLES ▲ 1775–1778

18
Guilford Courthouse, NC
March 15, 1781
Last major victory for the British in the South.

19
Yorktown, VA
September 28–October 19, 1781
General Washington led the Continental Army, joined by French naval and land forces, to defeat the British army led by General Cornwallis, who surrendered. Americans won the Revolutionary War.

16
Kings Mountain, SC
October 7, 1780
First significant patriot victory in the South, forces led by Francis Marion, nicknamed "Swamp Fox."

4
Moore's Creek, NC
February 27, 1776
Early in the war, this was the first battle won by patriot forces.

17
Cowpens, SC
January 17, 1781
Another victory for the American forces over the British.

15
Camden, SC
August 16, 1780
The Continental Army suffered a major defeat after a British surprise attack.

☐ American Victory   ☐ British Victory   ☐ Tie

Now many years later, our hearts full of pride,
With our fellow Americans here at our side,
The twilight is gleaming with red, white, and blue,
Giving proof through the night that our dream has come true!

For out in the distance—oh say can you see?—
It's America's future—its great destiny!
We leave it with you, with your hearts pure and strong,
For we have faith in you—and we have all along!

And you know, with a friend, there's no way you can fail
If he lends you a hand—or lends you his tail—
Together, you might change the world, just you see!
We did it together, my friend Thomas and me!

The Tail End
Resources for Parents and Teachers

Fourth of July in Virginia

Some Americans began celebrating the Fourth of July, Independence Day, in 1777, just a year after Thomas Jefferson and other members of the Continental Congress approved the Declaration of Independence. By the time of this story, nearly 50 years later, many communities and states observed it. The parade in the illustration is set in Charlottesville, Virginia, on the grounds of the University of Virginia, which Jefferson founded. Jefferson grew up near Charlottesville; he built his home, Monticello, outside of Charlottesville.

About the time of the American Revolution, British soldiers called American soldiers "Yankee Doodles." The Redcoats meant it as an insult; they considered the Americans poorly dressed backwoods fools. But the colonists quickly adopted the phrase as their own as a point of pride, throwing it back at the British—especially after the patriots began to match and beat them in battle!

Jamestown

The first permanent English colony in the New World began as a business opportunity. In 1606, King James I of Great Britain awarded a royal charter to the Virginia Company of London to start a colony in America. The company hoped to make money from harvesting and trading the resources there—in particular, gold. In 1607, more than 100 men arrived in the Chesapeake Bay and established Jamestown on the James River, named for the King.

Early life in Jamestown was difficult. The leadership of Captain John Smith helped the colonists survive, as did his friendship with the local Indians, the Powhatans. Pocahontas was a member of that tribe. The colonists' activities included brickmaking, glass-blowing, and making pottery; they did not find any gold. But Virginia became a strong and successful colony because of tobacco farming and exporting.

The Tail End
Resources for Parents and Teachers

Thirteen Colonies

Throughout the 1600s and 1700s, more people came from Britain to the eastern coast of North America to settle. Some colonies, like Jamestown, were established as part of a business opportunity. People seeking new, safe places to practice their religious beliefs established others, like the Plymouth colony in Massachusetts.

English colonists expected to enjoy the same rights as their fellow citizens back home in Britain, where a legislative body that included elected representatives, the Parliament, represented the people and worked with the King to govern the country. By 1760, every colony had a provincial legislature that allowed for some self-government; each assembly worked with a royal governor appointed by the King. But the colonists had no representatives in Parliament.

★ ★ ★

The Stamp Act

In the 1750s and 1760s, Britain and France were at war in North America over which country would dominate it and its rich resources. France was helped in the fighting by some Indian tribes; many colonists, including a young George Washington, fought alongside the British as subjects of the King. Britain won, but the war left it with heavy debts.

The King and Parliament decided to assert more control over the colonies and, without their input, to tax them more. One new law prevented colonists from moving farther west; another raised taxes on sugar to help pay for the colonies' defense. These steps upset many colonists. But in 1765, Parliament angered them even more by passing the Stamp Act, which taxed shipping, tavern licenses, newspapers, and other products and services through the sale of special stamps. The colonists began to protest in the streets and to boycott English goods.

The Tail End
Resources for Parents and Teachers

Boston Tea Party

Tensions continued to rise in the colonies as the King's government adopted other oppressive policies. Parliament imposed new taxes on the colonists for lead, paint, paper, and tea imported from England. Violence erupted in 1770 when British soldiers—Redcoats—fired on a crowd of rock-throwing protestors in Boston, killing five of them. The incident became known as the Boston Massacre.

In December 1773, continued colonial anger over taxes on tea led a group of Boston patriots to dress up as Indians, board three ships at night, and dump cases of tea into the harbor. This outraged the British government, which responded with more restrictive laws that the Americans called the "Intolerable Acts."

★ ★ ★

First Continental Congress

After Parliament passed the Intolerable Acts and other tough laws, the colonies began to oppose British policies more forcefully and work more closely together. Representatives of all the colonies except Georgia met in Philadelphia in 1774 for the First Continental Congress. They demanded Parliament repeal the Intolerable Acts and other legislation and, by meeting, took a big step toward united self-government. In addition, the Continental Congress approved resolutions to make military preparations for a possible British attack on Boston.

The Tail End
Resources for Parents and Teachers

Concord and Lexington

The people of Massachusetts prepared to fight the British. They gathered weapons and ammunition. Farmers and townspeople trained as "Minutemen," citizen-soldiers ready to fight on a minute's notice. British army commanders learned that the colonists were storing a large supply of gunpowder in Concord, just outside of Boston. On the night of April 18, 1775, the commanders sent about 1,000 Redcoats on the road to Lexington and Concord. The next day, Redcoats and Minutemen met and fought in and around the towns, including on a bridge. The first shots fired were the "shots heard round the world," for they marked the first battles in the American Revolution—and America's march to freedom and independence.

★ ★ ★

Thomas Jefferson Writes the Declaration of Independence

The Second Continental Congress met in Philadelphia in May 1776. In June, delegates from Virginia proposed a resolution of independence. Congress did not act on it right away; instead it appointed a committee to draft a formal declaration of independence that would explain the colonists' reasons and justification for breaking away from Great Britain. The committee included Benjamin Franklin of Pennsylvania, John Adams of Massachusetts, and 33-year-old Thomas Jefferson of Virginia. In a room in a house at Seventh and Market Streets, Jefferson wrote the draft in 17 days with the assistance of Franklin and Adams.

Jefferson was not only a great leader, he was also an architect and inventor. In the illustration, you will find five things that Jefferson invented: the clock, the bookstand, the portable desk, the swivel chair, and the "stand up" desk."

The Tail End
Resources for Parents and Teachers

Presenting the Declaration to Congress

Jefferson and the other members of the committee sent the draft Declaration to Congress on June 28, 1776. On July 2, delegates voted for independence from Great Britain; then they began debating, considering, and reviewing the Declaration itself. They made some changes to it but basically agreed to most of Jefferson's wording.

The document consisted of four main sections:

The first section is the **introduction**. It states that when a group of people decides to form its own country and government, the people should "declare" to the world their reasons—their "causes"—for taking such a big, important, and difficult step.

The second section is the **preamble**. It lays out the principles—the "self-evident" truths—that the patriot leaders embraced to take this drastic action, including that "all men are created equal" and are "endowed" by God with "certain unalienable rights," including "life, liberty and the pursuit of happiness."

The third section is the **body**. It lays out the colonists' complaints against King George III and his Parliament, "a long train of abuses and usurpations." The "facts submitted to a candid world" include invading the colonies, cutting off their trade, taxing them unfairly, and ignoring their requests for help and relief.

The fourth section is the **conclusion**. It says that because of all of this mistreatment, the colonies "are, and of right ought to be free and independent states" and that their political connection to Great Britain is "totally dissolved."

One of the issues the delegates argued about was slavery. Jefferson's draft included a paragraph condemning slavery and slave trading. By 1776, the colonies had imported hundreds of thousands of slaves from Africa; they worked mainly in southern colonies on farms and plantations. Because the southern colonies relied so heavily on slave labor for farming, this section of Jefferson's draft was eliminated from the final version to win southern support for the document. Historians find Jefferson's attack on slavery odd, as he was a Virginia farmer who himself owned slaves.

The Continental Congress voted to adopt the final version of the Declaration in the early morning hours of July 4, 1776.

The Tail End
Resources for Parents and Teachers

The Signers: 56 Men

The 56 representatives of the 13 colonies at the Continental Congress in the summer of 1776 were lawyers, doctors, merchants, and farmers. The signers included the primary author of the Declaration of Independence, Thomas Jefferson, as well as the delegates who assisted him, Benjamin Franklin and John Adams. John Hancock of Massachusetts, the president of the Congress, signed first and wrote the biggest, boldest signature. Another signer was Button Gwinnett, a Georgia plantation owner.

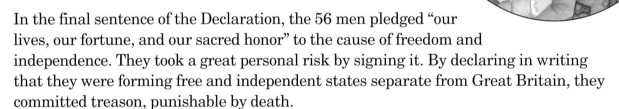

In the final sentence of the Declaration, the 56 men pledged "our lives, our fortune, and our sacred honor" to the cause of freedom and independence. They took a great personal risk by signing it. By declaring in writing that they were forming free and independent states separate from Great Britain, they committed treason, punishable by death.

★ ★ ★

Independence Hall: Reading the Declaration

After the Continental Congress approved the Declaration, church bells rang throughout Philadelphia in celebration. Congress ordered copies printed and distributed to various colonial assemblies, committees, commanders of the Continental Army, and others. Local officials read the Declaration aloud in many communities to cheers.

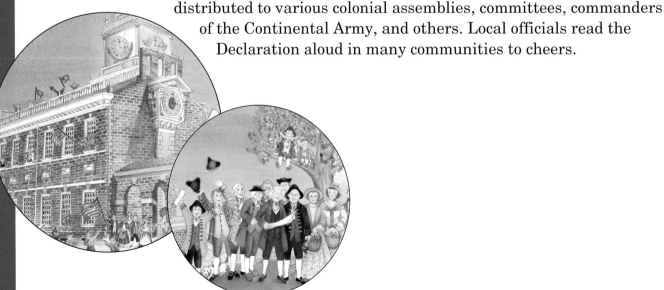

The Tail End
Resources for Parents and Teachers

Revolutionary War Battles

The Revolutionary War was well underway by July 4, 1776. The Declaration of Independence simply formalized the American rebellion against Great Britain. The first battles had occurred in Lexington and Concord more than a year earlier. The Continental Congress had created the Continental Army in June 1775; it had appointed George Washington as commander-in-chief. (Washington did not attend the Second Continental Congress or sign the Declaration of Independence because he had resigned from Congress and was leading patriot forces in the defense of New York City at the time.) State and local militias fought the Redcoats as well. From the first clashes in 1775 to the patriot victory in Yorktown, Virginia, in October 1781, the colonists fought more than 1,000 battles against British forces, some big and some small.

★ ★ ★

Celebrating the Fourth of July

While states and communities celebrated Independence Day in large and small ways from the start of the Revolution, Congress did not approve the Fourth of July as an official federal holiday until 1870. By 1776, fireworks were a part of many colonial celebrations—so much so that on July 3, the day before the Continental Congress formally approved the Declaration, John Adams wrote to his wife Abigail that Independence Day would be the "most memorable in the history of America. I am apt to believe that it will be celebrated by succeeding generations as the great anniversary festival. It ought to be solemnized with pomp and parade, bonfires and illuminations (fireworks) from one end of this continent to the other, from this time forward forever more."

Acknowledgments

We wish to acknowledge and thank our "art angels,"
Kappy Prosch, Vicki Malone, and Eva Marie Ruhl, who took many of
Cheryl's black and white ink drawings and turned them into vibrant,
colorful illustrations. A special thanks to Catherine Armour
and Leslie Exton of the Corcoran College of Art + Design
for introducing us to our "art angels." An extra special thanks
to Eleanor Reed's writing and editing expertise. (They all get an "A+"!)
We also want to thank Marji Ross of Regnery Publishing and
Jeff Carneal of Eagle Publishing for giving us our second chance
by believing in our books and their message
to Little Patriots everywhere.

—PWB and CSB